Bert
Smells

Hello.

I am Real Bert. I do not live on a farm and I am not sure what a rabbit actually is, but I have been lost once. I now have two humans, a soft bed and live outside London. I think I am ten. I do not smell. Much.

My humans got me from Mayhew, an animal welfare charity in North London, where I had been looked after by a lovely foster family after being found abandoned on the North Circular ring road. The North Circular is horrible at the best of times, but worse when you are just left there. That was the time I was lost I mentioned earlier.

This story is a work of fiction. Names, characters, events and incidents are the products of one or other of my humans' imagination. Any resemblance to actual dogs (apart from Me), rabbits, squirrels, pigeons, cows, rats, mice and foxes, living, dead or imagined; or to actual events (apart from Me) and incidents is purely coincidental.

Thank you.

Bert
September 2020

Bert
Smells

(Oh yes, he does.)

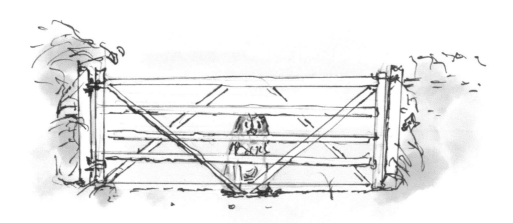

Published by weasle.art Limited

Text © Richard Revill, Suzanne Cole writing as P.A.Weasle

Illustrations © Richard Revill

First published by weasle.art Limited, Claygate, 2020

weasle.art Limited, Reg No. 12951499

ISBN: 9798686433014

This story is about Bert.

Bert lives on a farm which has a warm bed with toys and a warm fire and a loving family and a gate.

But Bert smells. Bert smells things and Bert smells of things.

Each morning, Bert gets up, has his breakfast and does his rounds.

"First, I'll roll in cool, wet stuff," he gruffed to himself.

"Then I'll roll in dry, dusty stuff," he huffed to himself.

"Then I'll roll in the grass around the back where the farm meets the wild, which is especially good for the smell of fox," he wuffed to himself.

"And, finally, I'll finish it all off with the stinky mud by the compost heap in the brown, green, slimey place behind the kitchen."

And when he smells just right and the flies have all arrived, he goes off to check that the fences and the walls and the railings and the hedges all smell just as they also should.

And did we mention the gate?

On this day, the gate was not shut. It was not shut at all. In fact, it was wide open! Beyond it there were new, new irresistible smells.

Bert knew he should not go out of the gate on his own, but the smells were just too much.

"Hello gate," said Bert as he strolled through, pretending to be going nowhere.

"Just passing," he added, pretending not to sniff.

The gate was silent, it didn't even squeak.

Bert follows his nose past the hedgerows and the brambles.

Bert's nose leads him under the first tree down the lane after the hedgerows and the brambles.

"Hey, Squirrel, how you doing?" called Bert from the ground.

"Fine. Fine. Absolutely fine. Can you smell something? I can. Not nice. Not nice at all," said the squirrel.

"That's me," said Bert, "that's how I smell."

"Vile," gulped the squirrel, dropping his nuts.

Bert's nose leads him under the second tree down the lane after the first tree down the lane after the hedgerows and the brambles.

"Hey, Pigeon, how you doing?" called Bert, sniffing the air.

"Lovely, apart from your awful smell, my dear," said the pigeon.

Bert's nose leads him past the bank after the second tree down the lane after the first tree down the lane after the hedgerows and the brambles.

"Morning rabbits," said Bert, sitting down.

"Phew!, Whiffy!" squeaked the younger rabbits who hadn't learned to be polite yet, "You smell!" they chorused.

"Thank you," said Bert, "new on today."

Bert's nose leads him past the big field after the bank after the second tree down the lane after the first tree down the lane after the hedgerows and the brambles. It was all getting quite confusing.

"Hello, Cow," said Bert, as he had a scratch.

"Very pungent today, Bert," moo-ed the cow.

"Thank you," said Bert, "newly rolled in."

The fields became houses, the lanes became roads, the hedges became walls, and the silence became noise.

Bert's nose leads him on and on and, soon, after the underpass and the puddles and the skips and the bins, Bert was farther from the gate than he'd ever been.

"Oi, mate! You don't smell from round here, no, you most certainly do not smell from round here," shouted a disgusting rat from a disgusting drain.

"I might be a bit lost," said Bert

"Well, you'd better keep going then. Don't want to hang around here like a bad smell, eh?" the rat's laugh became a wracking, unhealthy cough.

Bert's nose carried him on, but, in truth, he didn't know where he was and didn't know the way home at all.

"Excuse me, do you know my way home?" asked Bert of a family of young mice in a pizza box.

The mice all held their noses and pointed in different directions.

"Poo!" they all shouted, "You smell really bad!"

It started to get dark and began to rain, and Bert sat down under a big blue sign that didn't smell helpful at all. He was very sad now. No-one would help him because he was so smelly.

Bert dreamed of his home and how happy he had been. The rain got heavier and Bert got even sadder.

"Hello?"

Bert woke up. It was night time, and in the moon, he could just make out a slim shape.

"Hello? Can I help you? You are lost, yes?"

And now Bert saw it was a beautiful fox.

"Yes, I am lost and I can't find my way back to my gate. And no-one wants to help me because of my smell."

"But it has rained. To me you do not smell bad. You remind me of my family far away."

She swished her beautiful, bushy long tail and looked over the pizza boxes, crisp packets, discarded cans and cartons, out across the ring road.

"I know your gate. Come with me!" and she set off.

Bert followed her past the mice's pizza box.

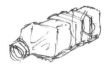

Bert followed her past the rat's drain.

Bert followed her past the cow's field.

Bert followed her past the rabbits' bank.

Bert followed her past the pigeon's tree.

Bert followed her right up to his gate in the hedgerow with the brambles.

And then...

The fox was gone.

"Thank you," said Bert, to the moon and the night sky.

"My pleasure," he heard her say, "You smell nice to me. I will watch over you always."

End Note:

We would like to give our heartfelt thanks to the Mayhew Animal Home for introducing us to, and allowing us to adopt, Bert. Without Bert, Richard would not have started drawing again, and we would not have written this book. He has been an inspiration; so, Mayhew, thank you, thank you, for the work you do.

In their own words:

Mayhew works to promote animal welfare by delivering a broad range of community-based veterinary, care and education services in the UK and overseas. We want to share our point of view to inform and change behaviours, and improve animal welfare. We take a realistic view of the - often difficult - situations that pet owners face, and look for ways to reduce the number of animals in need through pro-active initiatives and preventative care. We know that a major part of our work is in understanding the links between social issues and animal welfare. We do not judge. We listen. We value people too. Find out more at themayhew.org .

Printed in Great Britain
by Amazon

51659974R00015